EL IF

(U N T R U E)

B O O K O N E

EL IF

(U N T R U E)

B O O K   O N E

QUESTION ARC

ANTHONY PYTHON

EL IF (UNTRUE): BOOK ONE

QUESTION ARC

© 2019 ANTHONY PYTHON

All rights reserved.

O N E

---

*P*anting and breathing hard, Kira woke up from her slumber. In her little construction, which looked more like a tin can than a house, she was awoken by the rattling sound of metal scraps collapsing on each other. *That is not a good sound.* Everything had been quiet since the last fleet of robots passed, which was two days ago. Whenever the robots came around, there was the cry of despair that heralded the presence of these robots.

Everyone ran into their hideouts to keep themselves from being taken by these robots. These robots carried out experiments on human beings with a basic plan to understand the human brain and how it worked such that they may construct an artificial intelligence that operated in the similitude of the complexities and superiority of the human mind.

Kira kept silent as the robots walked by. She could hear the sounds of the metallic feet of the robots, knocking against everything in their way. Right where Kira was hidden, her mind drifted off to when life was beautiful. In those days, the fields were green and the environment was not in ruins; until the system was built two years ago.

Within two years, everything had been burned down. The streets were deserted and the green fields were uncared for. Destruction had come upon the city by the hand of man's creation. Man's creation had decided to take over the ownership of the earth from its maker.

All of a sudden, the sound of silence snapped Kira out of her reverie. She peeped through the window and saw that they had left. Like meerkats from the tunnel, everyone began to emerge from their hideouts. She heaved a sigh of relief and stepped out of her little home. Kira was a beautiful lady with green eyes and a long green hair that was typical of her. Ever since the beginning of the war, she had barely had time to dress up. She preferred being smartly dressed in her black shorts and black knee high boots, in case there might be a need for her to run for her life.

"Wow. They are beginning to show up more often that they normally do," Latoya—Kira's neighbour and friend—said. Latoya was in the military before everything fell apart. She was a proud black woman who enjoyed going on and on about the popping melanin in her skin. She was a tall woman, always wearing an afro. She was a real live embodiment of beauty and brawn.

"I wish we appreciated what we had those days. Then we would go to work and have parties and live in comfortable homes. Right now, we live in these things," Kira said, scornfully waving her hand at the metallic structure in which she lived. "Hardly do we get good food and clean water."

Latoya shook her head. "Those hideous things rained fire and burned up everything. Something has to be done."

"Who would do something? These things are in charge of the government. We are doomed if we sit on our asses," Kira puffed.

"Baby girl, what are you going to do about it?" Latoya asked.

"I almost finished building the stuff I told you about," Kira said gleefully.

"Girl, you're crazy. There are so many crazy stuff in your head. So, tell me the one that you built," Latoya inquired.

"I told you about the idea I got, concerning building the device that totally destroys the robots. I told you, right?" Kira asked.

Latoya slowly moved her head from side to side, as she wore a very weird look on her face that suggested that she felt Kira was being stupid. "No! You didn't tell me anything that ridiculous," she responded.

Kira continued, "Well, now I have. I have almost built it. It is about 95 percent complete. At the flick of the button, a sound wave is sent across that resonates at the frequency of the robot's board, thereby shattering it immediately."

"Ok. So why is it not completed?" Latoya asked sarcastically.

"I can see your disbelief. It is so palpable. Anyway, I just need one more thing—a robot's head," Kira responded with a displeased look washing over her face, as she looked down.

Latoya cleared her voice. "I might be able to help with that."

Kira's face lightened up like the face of a kid that saw gifts under the Christmas tree on the morning of Christmas. "What did you just say? Do you mean it?"

Latoya rolled her eyes. "You are in luck. I found a robot part and I decided to wheel it in. I didn't know that it was going to be useful someday. It is in my shed right now."

"Let's check it out now," Kira shouted as she began running towards Latoya's little building.

On arriving at the little house which was not far from Kira's tin can, Latoya entered the house—more like a shed—and brought out the part of the robot. It happened to be the exact part that Kira needed. The part Latoya found was made of the upper body part of the human-like robots but it had no limbs.

"Latoya, you have made me a happy woman. I love you darling," Kira said and tried to hug Latoya.

Latoya shut her a face. "Don't hug me. That stuff better be working. Get to work immediately and stop tryna hug me."

Kira responded, "Right away lady." She ran out of Latoya's house and headed to her tin can and began finishing the process of building her machine.

Just before everything fell apart some few years ago, Kira was a very established engineer. She had dabbled into quantum physics and electrical engineering. Most of the knowledge that she had gathered from her areas of expertise were becoming very useful, even in these difficult times. She used to be a very popular scientist and speaker, who spoke at different seminars in the United States.

Often times, she had battled with having to explain to men that she got to her career heights by focusing on her dreams and her work. However, they were difficult to convince. They felt what was working for her was her beautiful face and her curvy body. Now that the United State had been reduced to something below the shadow of itself, she clearly felt she had made her point by surviving thus far without the help of anyone.

Exactly two years before the devastation, she was reached by a particular professor whose name was Charles Rogers. He had decided to embark on a project that was going to be ground-breaking and he needed the best hands on it. On a particular Monday afternoon, he had invited her out for lunch. Kira had never seen him before, apart from when they charted online about work. As a result, she had insisted that they met in an open place, which was just round about a corner from where she worked.

On arriving, she was met by Charles, who was an impressive young man with slightly grey hair. He had blue eyes that made it seem like the ocean poured out of his eyes. He was actually more good looking than she could have imagined. Kira was hoping that this could go from a meeting about work to an opportunity to set time for another date.

"Charles?"

"Yes, I am Charles. It is my utmost pleasure to meet you in person Kira." He gave a handshake that was just perfect. It was not too tight or too loose. It was just perfect!

"I hope I was not rude earlier when I asked that we met in a public place. It is difficult to trust these days," Kira said calmly.

"Nope. It is fine. I understand completely. I may have done the same if I were in your position." He extended his hands, directing Kira to take a seat by his side. "Please, have your seat."

Kira was impressed by his politeness. "Yes, may we get to work quickly," she said, trying desperately to hide the fact that she loved what she saw.

"Alright then. I am building a computer that serves as a major server to many other computers. The real purpose of this is to build a society where humans beings have enough time to focus on every other part of their lives while the other computer, which will be robots and AIs take the less important jobs in the society. Therefore, the server would be broadcasting to the robots about what it needs them to do per time. The system would be built with its own, almost-human intelligence, such that nobody has to worry about the system because it would work perfectly by itself," Charles explained.

For a minute, Kira had forgotten that she was drooling over Charles some minutes ago. She had found the idea so fascinating that she was almost blown away, until a quick question dropped in her mind. "What jobs are less important?"

"Is it not best that everyone had time for other things and experienced complete happiness in life? Not having to wake up to attend to any job may give you the joy you desire. The robots can get to do all the menial jobs, like sales, cleaning of the home, sweeping of the roads. And, the system I am building would be able to control all of that," Charles further explained.

Right where Kira was seated, she could not stand the thought of the many loopholes of this idea. *How do people make money then? Complete replacement of humans by androids suggests that there will be an increase in crime rate. What if the androids, since the system that controls the androids will have almost-human intelligence, turn on us?* In order not to sound rude she had to come up with an excuse to not be part of the project. The project seemed good but she feared what it would lead to. "Sadly, I would love to be a part of this project but I have to go on a particular tech seminar on behalf of my company. I may be away for a year in Britain. I cannot be half in."

"What if I asked that you resign? I would pay more than twenty times what you're being paid," Charles boasted.

"I…I find that generous of you," she stuttered. "But I love where I am."

"I guess it was worth the try," Charles smiled.

"Thank you for considering me. I appreciate that," Kira smiled, picked her bag and headed back to her office, after she had appropriately disposed him.

Some few weeks later she saw a report on the television, with Charles speaking concerning the progress they had achieved in their new technological breakthrough. Some few months after, his creation turned on him, killed him and began a mission to take over earth. Also, the main system wanted to enjoy the fullness and beauty of being human and having the human mind. This lead to the human abduction and experimentation. As a result of the system's persistence in human execution, it was renamed M.A.X, which was an acronym for Maximize Assured Extermination.

This system had turned on humanity and had brought the apocalypse closer than everyone hoped. Kira had envisioned this; therefore, she was not particularly caught unaware.

Now, working in her little house, she tested her creation on the board of the robot that she had gotten from Latoya. Her assumption was right. The connection board of the robot just shattered without hesitation. Kira smiled. She had accomplished her dream. *You shall be named the Resonating Sound Device,* she said to herself.

T W O

The system had successfully created a community within itself, such that AIs were recreated, by the system, to be personalities. These personalities were totally different from the robots or androids that collected human beings for testing and elimination.

The robots that abducted human beings were outside the system—in the human world—and got their instructions from these human-like AIs within the system. These AIs were laden with the responsibility of carrying out some particular program functions, all for the proper functioning of the system.

Dent Ashdown, being one of the AIs, created to have the outlook of a bald middle aged man, hated his job. His work was to handle disk defragment. Often, he was looked down on by other AIs who considered his job irrelevant. Every morning, he woke up wondering what the world outside the system would be like.

All he had seen since he was created was the community of AIs that had been created to have the likeness of humanity but lacked the desire to socialise. Other AIs within the community had their minds always focused on what they had to execute; however, Dent had a lot of time on his hands. The availability of time got him desiring socialisation, which was a malfunction in his actual configuration. He could not explain this desire but he was sure that his heart was desiring something that other AIs could not comprehend.

As a result of this, he had tried, more than once, to raise discussions with other AIs but every time, he met a steel wall. Hence, he was really hated by everyone.

On a particular day, he woke up to carry out his usual early morning routine. Everything seemed dull. That day seemed like an extension of the day before because he woke up exhausted and burdened by the thought of getting to work that day. Struggling out of bed, he grabbed the jar into which he urinated, although the bathroom was some feet away.

Fighting the desire to remain in bed, he hurled himself to the bathroom and took his shower. After he had taken his shower, he rushed to make some cooked eggs which he preferred making in a waffle iron. Immediately he was done with breakfast, he hurriedly wore his white shirt and picked up a tie that was obviously out of fashion. The tie was a very big black tie with orange diagonal stripes. He wore his Tan Khaki pants, his black shoes and headed out of his home.

Dent worked in the archive. This particular day as he opened the archive, from where he gathered the files that seemed unneeded and fragmented and made them into one piece, he saw a cute dog called MAWL. Apparently the dog had been in a chamber, at the extreme end of the archive, called unwanteds A day before, he had left the unwanteds chamber open, letting the dog stray out of the chamber. This dog was an old software that was used to interpret action's in memory to the user. Simply said, it translates computer language to English language. She had been condemned to the archive when the system replaced it with an upgrade. She was left there, in the archive, to deteriorate.

What are you cute thing doing here?

The beautiful female dog whined softly as Dent held her in his hands. Dent was happy; his mood lightened up. The day which had seemed uneventful had become very eventful for him. He had always desired a companion and this little dog seemed perfect.

Returning to his table with the fluffy creature, he received a call. "Hello sir."

A strong voice that seemed very uninterested in having a friendly conversation with Dent replied, "I need you to get to search through the archive for fragments of a file and make it into one big file for me. The file is very important."

"What file sir?" Dent asked innocently.

"Just come over to my office. I can't speak over the phone," he replied and before Dent could say anything in response, the line went dead.

Dent was about heading to his boss' office with MAWL in his arms but he felt strongly that in this place where such acts of social interaction was hated, it would be stupid for him to carry the dog along. *I will be right back*, Dent mused.

Within some few minutes, he already arrived at the management where his boss' office was situated. He arrived before the door of his boss' office that had his name written on it in very bold letters—SAM DEERCOT. Dent knocked, twisted the handle and opened the door. "You sent for me."

Sam responded coldly, pointing Dent to a part of the PDF document that he needed him to work on. "There it is."

Dent picked the document and found the first word of the page of the document very fascinating to him "This is interesting," he said.

Sam stared at him shockingly. "May I know why you are trying to hold a conversation with me when you should be working?"

"I just wanted to know what the book is about," Dent replied with a frown on his face. He was disgusted by how Sam was speaking

"That is not part of your business. All you need to do is to gather the fragments of the folder and then get it converted to Word document and that's all. Get out," Sam spoke rudely.

Dent wanted to snap at him but he figured that he had so much to lose. He turned around and stepped out of the office. On heading to the archive, he read the first line of the file again. *Outside what we call reality is a reality, ruled by humanity. We would not stop until we become like them. Truly, the beauty of these unintelligent creatures is amazing.* Reading those lines kept churning in Dent's mind. He had heard about the existence of another world beyond his but he never had an idea what it looked like and he desired to see beyond his present environment.

He had gathered that some decisions that were made within the system was affecting the world outside but he barely knew if these decisions were affecting positively or negatively. Although he was created within the system, he felt alien in his own home. Rather than being in the system, he would prefer to launch into the unknown human world. *Maybe it would better and more friendly than the life in the system,* he said to himself.

Arriving at the archive, Dent began to rummage through the folders that contained the PDF files in the archive. After some hours of searching madly through the archive, he found the other parts of the PDF. Arranging the parts in order of chapters, he was able to make a complete book.

With the whole book within his grasp, he found out that the book had more to say about humanity than he thought. However, he could not deny the obvious bias in the tone of writing. In line with the instruction that he was given, he took the file to one of the few people, who was never hostile to him.

The name of the lady was Cota Rab. In the system, her work was to handle conversion of files, especially documents, from one readable form to the other. "Dent, what may I do for you?"

"Sam needs this PDF file converted to Word file," Dent replied.

Cota collected the book and immediately smiled. "This book always shows up once in a while."

"Really, it does?" Dent was puzzled because he had never seen the book.

"Normally, the book is published so that there is reference for any one of us, who has an interest in the work being done in the laboratory and it gives an idea what human beings are," Cota replied, as she adjusted the sleeves of her suit that had slid up due to all the work she was attending to.

"So why do they need it now?" Dent inquired.

"Often, when they make research from the humans they abducted, they update the book. I guess they must have made a great discovery," Cota replied.

"Wow!" On the outside, he seemed surprised and impressed but on the inside, he was disturbed that nobody else was worried about this.

"Right, I am surprised too. I wonder what they discovered. Very soon the outside world will be ours completely," Cota gleaned.

"One question Cota, do these human beings die after they have been experimented on?" he asked, swallowing hard, scared that he would not love the answer he was going to get.

"Yes. They often end up dead," she replied dispassionately.

Dent had known Cota for a while and he knew she was not a mean person. She had just been brainwashed by the system into believing that killing and abducting humans was a pious idea. Dent had been oblivious to what was happening for years. He began to wonder if he was the only one that did not know. "How come I didn't know about this? Does everybody else know?"

"Nope. But are you really wondering how I know? Do you have the slightest idea of the number of documents and printed records of laboratory work that passes my table each day?" Cota twisted her mouth as she stared at Dent, letting the question sink in.

He shrugged. Noticing that she had finished with the file conversion, he picked up the document, struggled to leave a smile for Cota and headed to Sam's office.

Arriving at Sam's table, he dropped the Word document on the table and looked at Sam who was seated in his table, reading an article. Dent asked, "What should I do with the PDF document?"

Sam, barely lifting his eyes from what he was reading replied, "You can dispose the PDF. Its outdated."

"Okay then," Dent replied.

Sam waved him out.

Dent headed to his office in the archive. As he opened the door, MAWL ran to him. He picked the dog up; the dog licked his face. Dent smiled. He had not felt this loved in a while. He could barely believe that he met the dog earlier in the day.

Dropping the dog, he went into the inner chambers of the archive where the bookshelves were located. His plan was to drop the PDF file on one of the shelves. As he approached the shelves, he looked at the book in his hand and he began to rethink his decision. Again the first few lines of the book flashed on his mind. Dent changed his mind, turned around and headed towards his seat.

At his desk, he began to scan through the book and his eye caught a paragraph. *Weirdly, humans enjoy the comfort of a social group, which could be family, colleagues or peers. At the same time, the interaction of the human species with one another, within that social group breeds competition, which breeds negative emotions like jealousy, anger and dissension; yet they find comfort in having people around. To us, it is an unfathomable phenomenon.*

Dent found the paragraph very captivating. One of the things he desired happened to be a peculiarity of the human species. At that point, he figured that if he wanted to comprehend all that the book had to say, he was going to return to the beginning of the book. He dropped the book on his table and stared blindly at the wall.

His mind travelled, thinking about what it would be outside of the system. Everything there was made of metal and mechanical parts, except for AIs like him, who worked within the system. He had no idea what to expect but he was hell-bent on getting there, enjoying this unseen world and interacting with the human creatures.

As he kept going deeper in his reverie, MAWL barked at him, jerking him to life. Dent looked at the wrist watch on his hand. He had covered his shift and it was time for someone else to take over. He picked up MAWL on one hand and signed out with the other hand. After signing out, he picked the PDF and stepped out of the office. As he walked out, he met the person who was supposed to take over from him. Dent flashed him a smile but he responded coldly. Dent ignored him and walked home happily, hopeful that he was about to enter the next best phase of his AI life.

THREE

The device that Kira built had a signal detector in it. she figured that if she wanted to destroy these androids that were attacking humans, she had to be able to find them; she had to be able to detect their presence.

With the android sample that she obtained form Latoya, she could figure out the exact signal given off by the androids. She figured that any other signal that was not of the androids was most definitely a distress signal.

Kira ran to Latoya's house. "Hey Toya. I have built the machine."

Latoya replied incredulously, "Surprise me!"

Immediately, the device began to beep. It had discovered the presence of an android. Kira smiled confidently. "You are just in time for a demonstration. Follow me." Kira turned the beeping off but could still see a display of the position of the androids on the LCD display screen on the device.

Running out of Latoya's little construction, the two ladies ran towards the source of the signal, hiding behind rubble from dilapidated buildings and iron scraps that littered around. As they kept following the location of the android, they met themselves on a main road. It had been a while since either of the ladies had been there. The road was littered with remains of burnt cars and motorcycles.

Everywhere was deserted and dusty. It was obvious that the city had been taken over by something that threatened human life. For such level of chaos as could be seen on the main road, everyone was either dead or hiding.

Ignoring the decimation and destruction that engulfed them, they kept following the signal.

"Wait!" Kira whispered. In the daylight sun, she could see something shinning in the distance. She looked at the position of the android that they were hunting on her device and she was pretty sure that she had found her target. "There he is," she said.

Latoya chuckled. "He, why he? You man hater. It is an It."

Kira could not believe what she was hearing. "Are you seriously kidding me! Latoya, now?"

"Okay, let's focus." Latoya feigned a straight a face.

Kira began slowly approaching the object in the distance with Latoya following behind carefully. Kira had not had the opportunity to test the distance from which her weapon could gun down an android but this was her opportunity. In all they did, the android must not see them because the system saw through the eyes of any android. This implied that when one android saw them, every other android had seen them.

Stealthily approaching, Kira and Latoya hid behind a car that was just some feet away from the android. Ensuring that she was at a good vantage point, Kira targeted her machine at the android.

Ensuring that she had a good target, Kira pressed the trigger. A sound wave from the gun hit the robot and it began twitching, until it finally fell to the ground, making a loud clanging sound.

Latoya observed all that happened in silence. She was astonished. "It works."

Both ladies came out of their hiding place. Kira was not disturbed because she knew they were in the clear. If any android showed up in the area, her device would give a mild beep. "I told you it works perfectly. I needed you to have an experience so that next time you would always believe me when I talk."

"Can I borrow it?" Latoya asked.

"Hell no!" Kira snapped.

Latoya scoffed. "Anyway, what is it called?"

"Resonating Sound Device. RSD," Kira replied.

"What a long name!" Latoya rolled her eyes. "Let us just call it Resed."

"Hmmm...Resed is nice," Kira agreed.

"It has to be nice. I named it," Latoya smirked.

Both ladies walked home confidently. They had no fear that anything could attack them. Even if anything was in the area, they would know.

"From now on, we cannot be threatened by anything. If they try, they are going down," Kira claimed.

"Well said baby girl. Well said!" Latoya nodded in agreement.

F O U R

$\mathcal{I}$ t had been three weeks since Dent found the book. No day passed without Dent reading through the book.

After reading the book, he had devised his way of getting to the outside world. The last chapter of the book spoke about the ongoing research to uncover how to transfer the consciousness of an AI to the body of a human. As at the time the book was written, the research boasted of being able to create human body parts from it's constituent elements.

Dent arrived at work with a basic plan of gathering all the information he could get concerning the phase of the experimentation. *Cota Rab always has information for me*, he mused.

He dropped his bag and his pet in his office and headed straight to management to speak with Cota Rab. "Hey Cota," Dent greeted.

"Hi, what may I do for you?" Cota asked.

"Well...I want to know if the records from the laboratory is back," Dent asked.

"You seem so interested. Why?" Cota asked, doubting Dent's motive.

"We need to conquer these humans. I am passionate about it," Dent responded sarcastically, nodding his head frantically.

"Well, the laboratory has created a human body and they have found a way to transfer the consciousness of the system, into the body," Cota paused. "This means the system would rule the world like a human."

"What is the point?" Dent asked. "If we want to eliminate them, why do we wanna be like them?"

"We will not be like them Dent. We would be better than them." She gleaned. "We would have all of their strength and all of our strength. We would corrode their minds until they bow to us and submit to us that we may change them to one of us."

"Wow! What a plan!" Dent sighed. "Any ideas when the consciousness transfer will happen?"

"In five days," Cota Rab responded.

"What?" Dent was shocked.

"It's five, Dent," Cota assured

"That's good," Dent responded, hiding the fear and horror on his face. "I should head to the archive now. I may be needed there."

"Alright. Freedom is almost ours," Cota called.

"Yes it is..almost," Dent hesitated. Turning away, he returned to the archive, panting and puffing. The death of mankind bothered him more than he could explain. He settled in his chair and began to think.

As he was trying to think, MAWL crept up to him. Dent picked up his pet and began to stroke the fur. It was relaxing for him. Suddenly, he was hit by an idea. MAWL's function, before he was condemned to the archive, was to interpret computer language to the user.

All Dent needed was a person who he could communicate with in the human world but he had no idea if anybody had access to a radio or signal detector. *I don't even have a radio*, he said to himself.

Dent began to feel a serious pain in his head. He had overworked his mind so much that he was feeling hypoglycemic.

Weak and tired, he got off his seat and headed to the RAMBar, where he was going to have a can of soda.

At the bar, he sat at the counter and requested for soda. Where he was seated, three individuals walked in and sat on a round table. These men were in charge of different duties within the system. Buck, always looking scruffy in a black shirt and black pants with a very thick moustache that got every one giggling when he passed, was in charge of backup.

Gen, being a short bald headed man, made up for his looks by always dressing neatly and good. He was in charge of power management but he was often so neat that others felt he never did anything. Com looked unassuming. He always came to work in casual wears. He hated shaving his beards, as he felt it was his signature look. He was in charge of sending signals and information to the outside world.

Dent had come to have a cold drink but he was delighted that he was going to be getting more than that. Where he was seated, he could hear the conservation going between the three of them. Again, he noticed that they never discussed about each other's life, as a show of concern; instead their discussion and entire focus was work. Dent shook his head in disappointment. *Even amongst friends, there is no love, care or concern*, he murmured.

The three men waved at the bartender. Com spoke, "Serve us the usual."

These men were frequent visitors of the RAMBar; hence, the bartender already knew their favourites. The bartender brought their drinks and served each of them.

"We are just five days away," Buck said.

"It's a lot of work. The process may drain all the power," Gen pointed out, frowning at the gravity of work that awaited him.

"Cheer up. There is going to be enough work to go around for everybody," Com added.

"Speaking of what is going around, I hear of a human who has been destroying our androids," Buck said. "I discovered the news while I was backing up the communication files yesterday."

"Her name is Kira," Com said.

At this point, Dent's ears were very open. He was not going to miss any bit of information that fell out.

"Kira has become some kind of superhero. In the past few weeks, her fame has spread so much that many people find solace in her. Whenever any of our androids show up, they immediately radio her," Com said.

Noting that it was still during work hours, Dent figured that if Com was seated in the bar, there was probably nobody in his seat, overseeing the communication. He paid the bartender, rushed to his office to pick up MAWL and immediately stormed to the communication room.

Just as he thought, there was nobody at the console. Immediately, he sat at the chair of the console, wrote a message in computer language and made his pet to translate it to English language. After he had done all of that, he sent out the signal with the message in it.

Carrying his pet in one hand, he rushed out of the communication room. As he walked towards the archive, he could see the image of Com appear in the distance. Dent knew he was in trouble because he had nothing to do around the communication area.

Eventually, Com passed by him. "Hey you. What are you doing here?"

Dent spun around, acting like he was cut unaware. "Hey sir. My dog strayed. I have been looking for her. Eventually, I found her in this wing."

"You should keep that thing in place. Get a leash or something; it won't stray with that," Com advised.

"Kind sir, thank you. I should head to my workstation," Dent said.

"Yeah, you should." Com walked off, confidently strutting off into the communication centre.

Dent smiled. On getting to the archive, he packed his bags, arranged his documents, picked up his dog and went home.

FIVE

$\mathcal{I}$t has been three weeks since she created her machine. As a result, her fame had spread across the land. In fact, everyone had grown to see her as the saviour of the human race. Naturally, people gravitated towards her because she was a beacon of hope and safety.

The people gathered and built a camp around her. Kira did not expect that her machine was going to make people look up to her that much.

Seated in her house, trying to get some rest from the patrol she had earlier in the day, her machine began to beep. Immediately, Kira's eyes became clear of sleep. She reached for her machine and quickly looked at the signal. Something was strange. Whenever her machine went off like that she would check the machine to find the signal given off by the androids.

This time, the signal she was getting was a very different one. It was a broadcast from an unknown source. Accessing the signal, it came in as a message. She opened the message and it read: *Kira, my name is D and you are in danger. If you ever see this message, just reply via this same frequency.*

Kira did not know how to respond to the message that she had received. *Who are you?* Kira replied the text. She waited for hours to receive a response but nothing came back. disappointed and vexed, she discarded the message.

The next day, she received a response to her message about the same time she had received the message the previous day.

"I am an AI but I think something has gone wrong in my configuration that makes me feel for the human race. By the way, sorry for the delayed response. I do not get enough time to spend with the transmitter," the sender replied to her previous message.

Kira replied, "What do you mean by I am in danger?"

"There is a plan to totally annihilate humanity. In fact, a human body has been built for the machine to inhabit such that he will become a leader for the new race of humans. These humans will be those who submit to his rule and allow him to put an implant in them, such that he gets to control everybody. Anybody who does not submit to him will be killed," the sender replied.

"Wow! That is something," she replied. "How long do we have before all these things begin?"

"Four days Kira…Four!" the sender replied.

"I need your help then. What is your name?" Kira asked.

"My name is Dent Ashdown. I need to go now. Lets talk same time tomorrow." Dent's signal stopped broadcasting.

In her small house, surrounded by a lot of people, she felt alone this time. All that Dent had told her left her thinking if fighting the system was a wise decision. As she kept churning the thought within her heart, she heard a knock on the door.

"Yo, Kira. Step out!" Latoya called.

Kira stepped out of her house. "What is happening?"

"Someone told me that they saw an android around here," Latoya whispered.

"But that is not possible. My device would pick it," Kira responded.

"I think they have devised a way to by-pass the signal they give—something to cover the signal," Latoya suggested.

"You are probably right," Kira replied. "What can be done?"

"We may need to create a plan to set up a perimeter and have people monitoring the perimeter. How about the guns?" Latoya asked.

"Well, I was able to make handguns that emit the sound frequency that shatters the boards. I do not have enough resources and that is all I can handle," Kira replied.

"How many?"

"Just seven guns."

"Good. We will distribute that seven to the people that stay at the perimeter at every hour. As we can't trust Resed to give us the help we want, we can always depend on our eyes," Latoya suggested.

"It is fine," Kira replied.

Latoya stepped out to fix the things that she and Kira had discussed.

Everything was becoming exhausting for Kira. Hearing that the enemy had devised a way to block her from detecting their presence had brought heaviness to her heart. Also, the news that Dent had brought did not even make her any better.

In the night, Kira could not sleep. She was still barnstorming, thinking about the best way to fix the present situation they were. *Or should we just attack them?* She asked herself.

All the while, Kira had been fighting defensively, trying to keep her people safe. But this time, she sensed that she may need to go on the offensive side. If she did not take the fight to them, they would bring it to her and she may never be ready to face the fleet of androids that would rain down on her and her people.

While churning these thoughts, she heard a loud cry outside: *The androids are here.* Kira leapt out of bed and headed out immediately with her machine. Kira was not ready for the sight that greeted her outside.

About twenty androids formed a wall, pushing towards the settlement, shooting sporadically. The settlement was in disarray. These androids tore through houses and constructions, shooting anybody they saw.

Ahead, Kira saw one of the androids. As it turned to look at her, she hit the trigger. The android felt the sound wave that the gun sent across but it just shook it off and proceeded towards Kira.

Kira's pupils dilated. This was no longer a joke. These androids had not only devised a way to mask their signals; they had also changed their boards such that the sound wave could not shatter it any more.

Immediately, she turned around and ran off. The android did not stop chasing her. As she kept running, she found a crowbar in her path. She grabbed the crowbar and hid from the android.

The android stopped running, as it had lost her. Slowly, it kept moving through the pile of metal scrap that tiled the junk yard that Kira had run into.

Maintaining complete silence, Kira could see the approaching android, from behind the car she hid. Although it was dark, the android beamed lights from its eyes that helped Kira know where it was and the direction in which it was facing.

Suddenly, the lights went out. Kira began to weep quietly. At that point, she just wanted to step out of her hiding place and tell the android to kill her but she remembered that people depended on her. She was not even sure the situation that those people were but the thought of these people gave her the strength to stay strong.

A burst of light shone on Kira, blinding her completely. The android had found her. It grabbed her by the neck and raised her up with one hand. Kira swung her crowbar but the lack of oxygen had taken the energy out of her. She had began to choke and there was no miracle in sight.

"Hey you," Latoya called.

The robot turned to look at who called it but before it could see the caller, a big sledge hammer drove across the face of the robot. The lights went off and Kira dropped from its grasp.

"I am so happy to see you," Kira cried, hugging Latoya tightly.

"Well, this was how I killed the android that you used for your experiment. The hammer still works well," Latoya replied.

"How did you know I was here?"

"I had decided that it was important to keep an eye on you because the creation of that machine of yours puts a target on your back. Since then, I had taken it upon myself to watch you," Latoya said, trying to sound dispassionate as she could.

"I am special to you," Kira joked.

"Girl, shut up! Just focus on getting that machine to work. This is the new robot that you can use for experimentation, I guess you may just need to adjust the parameters," Latoya replied.

"How is everyone at the camp?" Kira asked, as Latoya helped her up.

"They are all probably hiding or have scattered all around," Latoya replied.

"It's late. We better just find a place to hide our heads," Kira suggested.

"I agree. This is a metal junk yard. It cannot be difficult to find a car that we can sleep till morning," Latoya said.

After a brief search, they found a car and rested in it till morning.

Some hours gone by, Kira woke up to behold the sun. Last night was so scary for her that it seemed like the next day was not going to come at all.

"Wake up Latoya," Kira said. The morning seemed to come with a new hope being shone on the heart of Kira. "We need to get to work."

Latoya woke up. After gathering herself for some minutes, they headed back to the settlement, with the robot being dragged along.

They arrived to meet other people who had fled the night before arriving too. Death reeked in the air. Bodies were lying around. Tears, cries and wails tore through the air. People cried for their loved ones that lay in a pile of blood.

Kira was sad and embittered. Now it had become real to her that not every war was won by being defensive; for some, you may need to be offensive. Tears trickling down her cheek, soon began to flow heavily.

"Kira. This people are dismayed and discouraged. They look up to you for hope. Now might be a time for you to encourage them," Latoya said.

Kira nodded in agreement but could barely speak with the tears.

"Alright then." Latoya raised her voice, waving her hands too, signaling that the people should gather round. "Hey, everybody. Gather round. Kira wants to speak to us."

Reluctantly, everybody gathered.

Kira coughed and began to speak. "Everything that has happened between yesterday and today has taught me a lot. We cannot win this fight by being scared. We created these things and we alone can take these things out. We cannot hide and be afraid any more. If we continue like that, they will always have the upper-hand. Therefore, I urge you to direct the anger and the pain to these androids. If we stand together, we would win. We would avenge our people, who have died by the hands of these things. From now, we are soldiers and every training we have had in the past has prepared us for this particular war. Until victory is ours, we are not resting. We would take this fight to the gates of the enemy."

Everyone hailed. Kira had given them hope. Although she found it difficult to even believe all she said, she had come to the resolve that no matter what happened, she won't back down until victory was won.

While others cleaned the settlement and everyone found a place to bury their loved ones, Kira focused on getting the machine to work appropriately.

She upgraded the machine such that it was going to be able to unmask the signal given off by the androids. Also, she was able to adjust the parameters such that the shock wave released by the the machine—Resed—would destroy both the old and the new androids.

The device beeped; a message came in. "I am sorry about last night's attack. I heard about it this morning. My heart is with you and your people," Dent wrote.

Kira was angry. Without so much of a thought, she replied, "I am not interested in talking to you. How sure am I that you are not the problem. You may even be the enemy. Just stop talking to me."

"I am not the enemy; I am your friend. Trust me. In two days time, the consciousness of the system will be passed into the humanoid they made. And I promise that he would wreck more havoc than these robots are wrecking. He would regenerate himself and take over all the human world. I advise that you hit the system unaware tomorrow. That is how we can win," Dent replied.

"You want to trick us into this trap. We would get there and all of a sudden your people would be ready," she responded.

"You have a choice. Trust me or die. However way it goes, I tried. I would try to fight for you from my side here but if you do nothing, it's all a a waste. I have a plan to steal the body but I need you to trust me." Dent stopped broadcasting.

Kira sat down on the cold floor in her house. She was tired, exhausted and confused. However, just like her gut warned her against creating system, her gut warned he to trust Dent. *My gut has saved me once; I will trust it again, this time,* she mused.

S I X

Dent had been thinking very hard on how to escape to the world outside.

Knowing that where was a body had left him considering nth idea of finding a way of throwing his own consciousness into the body.

He had studied Com's daily routine and he had found a perfect time to sneak into his office to send his messages to Kira and that helped his plan greatly.

The only way he could get into the body was to remove the consciousness that was installed on the chip that was to be put in the pseudo brain of the humanoid.

As simple as that sounded, it would be very difficult to achieve. The only way to get everybody so distracted was to ensure that a threat from outside had their attention.

Dent had also considered that it was best that he took over the body because the consciousness of the system would wreck havoc through it. Having so much time on his hand had given him the space to plan out his tactics very well.

At about midday, Dent was seated in his office. He knew his plan could not kick off if Kira did not attack the system from the outside. The discussion they had the day before was not convincing enough for Dent to believe that she was going to carry out the attack. Yet, he hoped and hoped greatly.

Suddenly, the power began to blink. He could hear people shouting outside his office. All of a sudden, the system was hit by a loud bang that caused everywhere to quake.

MAWL ran towards Dent; he smiled at her. *I have to live you now MAWL but I really will miss you and I will come back for you. You can't go where I am going*, Dent said to MAWL. The loud bang was the sign he was waiting for all along. Immediately, he ran out of his office and headed to the laboratory.

On arriving at the laboratory, he saw the body lying lifeless in a containment. He wished he could just jump into the body but it did not work like that.

The laboratory was empty. All the AIs in the laboratory had been diverted to focus on other matters as the system was under attack. The system paid little or no attention to security within the system because it was assumed that all the functional AIs in the system were on the same page, as their essence was from the system itself.

All of a sudden, a number of androids that were meant to put the consciousness into the human body entered the laboratory. They could not perceive Dent because he was a consciousness not a physical entity.

From their actions, he could deduce that they had been instructed to inject the consciousness of the system into the body.

The conciousness was supposed to pick the signals of the system and live like the system in human form. The conciousness itself was not alive but was just a receiver of the system's life.

The robots opened the channel through which the conciousness was going to be lowered into the brain of the body. As Dent could not be perceived by a physical entity, he crept into the channel as the robots tried lowering the consciousness into the brain.

As the conciousness was lowered into the brain, Dent slipped in along side. Dent decided that he would let the conciousness get activated in the body. He knew that if he interrupted now, they would detect that something was wrong.

As a result, he took a sit beside the receiver of the system's thoughts, in the brain of the humanoid. The androids hit the button that was beside the containment that the body was kept.

The system's consciousness immediately sent electric impulse through the body, jerking the body to life. It was a perfect body, built in the likeness and grandeur of the sculpted images of Zeus. Little did Dent know that the body had other powers and upgrades, which included its ability to know the thoughts of other people and its ability to fly. Also, it emitted laser rays from its eyes that could burn through titanium on impact.

The body broke out of its containment and suspended itself in the air. "You have done good, my servants," the body spoke gracefully to the androids. "Now lets go get this over with."

SEVEN

Kira obeyed the words of Dent. She had had to send out information and radio signals, calling for help from whoever could hear her. Surprisingly, she got a response from another clan of rebels who had been able to get their hands on some weapons that the military had left around. She had made an alliance with this other rebel group and they had gathered resources to fight against the system too.

Both groups attacked the system in its own community that it had created—a community of androids, working to serve the system and a very big facility that the system had built as its own home. They attacked with guns and bombs tearing the whole place up.

As much as they had tried to fight the androids, they were overpowered by these metallic creatures.

Suddenly, a creature that looked like a man, broke through the metallic walls of the system's home.

Immediately it broke out, the androids stopped fighting. It seemed as though the creature called them to pull back but without saying a word.

The humans began shooting at the creature but the bullet seemed to fall to the ground. The creature remained untouched and confident

Noticing how futile their attempts to destroy the man-like creature were, they stopped shooting.

"Humans," he, the humanoid, spoke loudly. "I am a creature like you. I am here to rule you. If you submit to me, I will let you go but those who stand against me will be utterly destroyed. Before we proceed, if you are on my side, move to this side and become a part of me...a part of us. If you don't wanna join us, then get ready to die."

After he had spoken, the people feared for their lives. They had had enough losses and they were not ready to entertain any more losses. One by one, the people dropped their weapons and joined the enemy.

Latoya turned towards Kira. "I am sorry Kira. We have lost so much this year and I am tired. Maybe they have good intentions; maybe we misunderstood them."

"What? You, Latoya? They attacked us, killed us, abducted our people and you think we misunderstood them?" Kira was shocked.

"Its better we join them than die!" Latoya yelled.

Kira responded, "Its better I die, than join them."

"So be it then. I love you." Latoya kissed her on the cheek and headed off to join the others on the side of the humanoid.

"Those of you who have found worth in life, that have decided to join me should climb into my glorious abode and await my glorious declaration of myself as the head of the new clan of super people. The rest of you be ready to die," he declared.

As they began matching into his abode, the others watched in horror. Dent figured that it was time to take over. He broke the device that transported the consciousness of the system to the mind of the humanoid.

The creature began to shout in pain. It began to writhe, screaming painfully. All of a sudden, everything stopped. The creature paused like it was being reprogrammed.

Whereas, the people who entered the facility in which the system was located, were locked in by the system immediately they got inside.

"Hello Kira," the creature called in front of everyone else. "My name is Dent. I have overridden the power of the system on this body. I am in charge now."

Kira was astonished as she heard a reassuring and friendly tone.

The system noticing that it had lost control of its weapon, the humanoid, the facility began to take off into the air. All the other people who had gone into the facility were trapped inside.

The androids on ground began to shoot at the humanoid. Within one sweep, Dent shot lasers out of his eyes that burned all the androids. He had ultimate power. The tides of the battle had shifted in favour of the humans. With the humanoid on the side of the humans, the victory was theirs already. The system, figured that destruction was imminent; therefore it had made an escape plan. And the plan was that the facility was going to take off if it was threatened, sending the system into outer space to prepare it for another strike.

The facility kept going up, until it disappeared out of sight, with the people on it. Dent and the rebellion cleaned up the city, destroying every one of the androids left.

When they had cleared the perimeter, Dent approached Kira. "Hello. Its I. Dent," he said sheepishly.

"Hey Dent. You look more handsome than I thought," she joked.

"Well, I look worse than this. They made me better." They both laughed.

"I know you don't trust me. Give me some time to prove myself to you," Dent asked, stopping Kira in her path.

"You don't have to do anything. You have done enough. You have fought for my people. And you have adopted my people as your people. All I need you to do is to clean this place for me. Let us together make it a better world. Let's work together in rebuilding and training our people for war if they ever came back," Kira said, with a fallen disposition. Her mind drifted to Latoya and all the people she had lost lately. All she desired was for everything to come to an end.

"I promise you that I am always here for you. When you need me, I would always be there," Dent said.

"That's fine. That is all I need," Kira responded.

In the weeks that followed, they spent the time putting structures in place and building a new world.